MARGIE AND ME

Beverly Wirth

Margie and Me

ILLUSTRATED BY
Karen Ann Weinhaus

FOUR WINDS PRESS
New York

Text copyright © 1983 by Beverly Wirth.
Illustrations copyright © 1983 by Karen Ann Weinhaus.
All rights reserved. No part of this publication may be
reproduced, stored in a retrieval system, or transmitted,
in any form or by any means, electronic, mechanical,
photocopying, recording, or otherwise, without prior
written permission from the Publisher. Published by
Four Winds Press, a Division of Scholastic Inc.,
730 Broadway, New York, N.Y. 10003.
Manufactured in the United States of America

10 9 8 7 6 5 4 3 2 1

The text of this book is set in 16 pt. Palatino.
The illustrations are half-tone drawings with overlays,
prepared by the artist for black, red, and yellow.

Library of Congress Cataloging in Publication Data
Wirth, Beverly.
Margie and me.
Summary: A young child finds a dog
in the playground and is allowed to keep her.
[1. Dogs—Fiction] I. Weinhaus, Karen Ann, ill.   II. Title.
PZ7.W774Mar 1983   [E]   82-21075
ISBN 0-590-07870-4

To Christina Rachael Kaiser

B. W.

For Samara

K. W.

CONTENTS

1
A New Friend

I saw you

in the playground.

You were lost.

You were hungry.

You were lonely.

You followed me home.

When Mother saw you,
she asked me
where I found you.
"In the playground," I said.
"How do you like
my new friend?"
Mother said she liked you,
but we could not keep you.
You had lost your name tag.
We had to help you
find your real home.

11

We tied a little rope
around your neck.

Mother and I took you
around to all the neighbors.
"Is this your dog?" I asked.

Nobody saw you before.

Nobody knew

where you came from.

15

When we got home,
I drew your picture.

We hung it in the post office.

Then Mother helped me
put an ad
in the newspaper.

It said,
"FOUND: One small brown dog
who is lost
and likes to lick a lot.
Call 233-4556."

I took you outside
and gave you a bath.
When I dried you off,
your hair was soft and shiny.

Father came home.

He petted you.

He asked me where I found you.

"In the playground," I said.
"How do you like her?
  Can we keep her?"
  Father said you were nice,
  but we could not keep you.
  It would not be fair.
  You were not our dog.

Then Mother and I gave you
some warm dinner.
You were really hungry.
You slept under my bed
all night long.
I didn't want you
ever to go away.

The next morning
we heard a knock
on our door.
It was a lady and a man.
The lady had a newspaper
in her hand.
She had seen our ad.
The man had my drawing
from the post office.

They said you were their dog.

I started to cry.

Then the man said,
"We are going away
on a very long trip.
And we do not know
when we will come back.
It will be hard
to take Margie with us.
She needs a new home."
"Would you like to have her?"
asked the lady.

I looked at Mother.

Mother looked at me.

"Yes," she said,

"we have wanted a dog

for a long time."

I gave you a big hug.

"We will miss Margie,"
said the man,
"but we are glad that she
will have a nice, new home."
The lady said,
"We love her very much.
We know you
will love her, too."
Mother shook hands
with the lady and the man.

"Good-bye," I said.

"Thank you for Margie!"

Then I took you inside.
And I said,
"Margie, you are mine.
Now you are all mine."

2
Margie Rides Again

I think you really like

to ride in the car, Margie.

When we go shopping,

you like to ride.

When we go to get gas,

you like to ride.

When we go to the library,

you like to ride.

But one day a bee

flew up your nose.

You tried to sneeze him out,

but he stung you anyway.

Then your nose

started to swell,

and swell,

and swell some more.

When we got home,
I put an ice bag on you.
It did not help.
I bandaged you up.
The bandage
did not help either.
That night
when you went out,
it was raining.
You stayed
outside all night long.

The next morning
when you came to the door,
you were all muddy.
When I washed you off,
your nose was much better!
Now you can go riding again,
Margie, you can ride again.

3

Margie Goes Away

You are my very
own dog, Margie.
I like to have you with me
all the time.
But one day I had to go
to the dentist.
You could not come.

Dogs were not allowed
in the dentist's office.
I patted you on the head.
I gave you a big kiss.
And I said,
"Margie, I cannot
take you with me.

You must stay at home.
I will be back soon."
Then Mother and I went
to see Dr. Miller.

We waited,

and we waited,

and we waited.

Finally Dr. Miller said

he was sorry to be so late

and to come in.

Then he cleaned my teeth.
He said everything was fine.
And he told me to come back
in six months
for another checkup.
Mother and I said
thank you and good-bye.

When we got home,
you were not there.
"Where are you, Margie?"
I called.
But you did not come.
I called again, louder,
"Margie? Margie?"
You were gone.

We looked everywhere for you.
You were not under my bed.
You were not in the big chair
in the living room.

You were not in the yard.
Maybe somebody stole you.

Maybe you got hurt
and need me
to help you.
Or maybe you are lost
and need me
to find you.

I knocked

on all the neighbors' doors.

Nobody had seen you.

I ran up and down the street,
crying, "Mar-gie,
Ma-a-a-r-g-i-e,
Ma-a-a-a-a-r-g-i-e!"
You didn't come,
and you didn't come.

Why did you go away?

Will you ever come back?

Where could you be?

Then I found you
in our favorite place,
the playground.
There you were
with a new friend!
Now you can
come home with me.
And you can
bring your new friend
with you, Margie;
he can come home
with us, too.